MW00872542

ISBN: 9798483803058
Published:2021

I AM...

21 daily affirmations
for children

Tashana Swaby – Scott

Zahira Scott

Zara Scott

For my Zahira and my Zara…

Always remember that

You are loved!

You are worthy!

You are children of God!

I AM...

A Child of God!

I AM...

Beautiful and Wonderfully made!

I AM...

Courageous

I AM...

Creative

I AM...

CONCERT

Excellence

I AM...

Unique

Made in the USA
Coppell, TX
19 November 2024